For Boris and Amanda, with whom we encountered the Pacifier Fairy for the first time.
And for Ava and Raphaël, who teach us about their imaginary world every day.

Pacita the Pacifier Fairy (Big Kid Chronicles, Book 1)
Copyright © 2020 Beyond the Bridge Communications, LLC
Cover & Book Design Copyright © 2020 Olivier Huette

Library of Congress Control Number: 2019950912 | ISBN-13: 978-1-7334568-0-7
Second edition: 2021. Printed in the U.S.A.

BISAC CODES: FAM025000 | JNF024050 | JUV039090

Published by Beyond the Bridge Communications, LLC, 1125, Spruce St. Berkeley, CA 94707. USA
bigkidchronicles.com

Pacita
The Pacifier Fairy

Charlotte Attry
Jeremie Febvre

Olivier Huette
Sophie Lawson

Somewhere far, far away, in a cute little shack,
Lives a quirky young fairy with a curious knack.

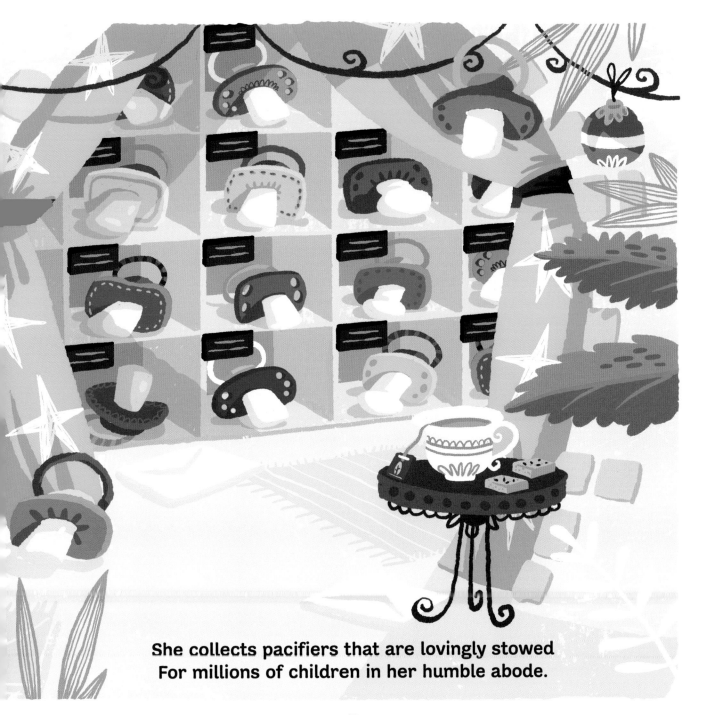

She collects pacifiers that are lovingly stowed
For millions of children in her humble abode.

Her name is Pacita and she's part make-believe,
Full of magic and mischief, with a trick up her sleeve!

She picks up the binkies to store for safekeeping,
And leaves warm-hearted letters while the children are sleeping.

9

At home as we grow, parents often point out,
To speak like a big kid, paci needs to come out.
Now it's time to move on and Pacita knows how.
"I'll look after your soothie" she says with a bow.

You'll lay out your binky, your heart heavy and tight.
That most precious of treasures, you'll tell it goodnight.

When you wake the next morning, you'll find in its place
A beautiful letter full of wisdom and grace.

Pacita has taken your dear friend on a trip,
But her compassionate words make your little heart skip.

She tells you to be proud and to trust in your choice.
Growing up can be hard but you'll soon find your voice.

Your paci will be kept with love and affection,
Becoming a part of her amazing collection.
Each one is precious and guarded with care,
In its own little cubby, exquisite and rare.

There might be some sorrow and a feeling of grief,
When you think of the binky who brought you relief.
Your family and friends will embrace you and say
"It's OK to feel sad" as they kiss tears away.

But Pacita is watching from somewhere close by,
Awaiting the moment when your eyes are all dry.
So a little while later, when you're feeling OK,
A second letter arrives to brighten your day.

"Congrats!" It says, "soothie's no longer needed!
The challenge seemed grand but you have succeeded!"

"From naptime and bedtime to trips in the car,
You're finished with paci, you've come so far."

After a couple of weeks, you'll happily find
Besides a few memories, it's out of your mind.
But if one day your pal pops back into your head,
Remember Pacita and the kind words you read.

ON THE PATH TO A LIFE WITHOUT PACIFIERS

It soothes, reassures, and consoles... But growing up means learning how to live without it. Here are some tools you can use to help your child let go.

⭐ ESSENTIAL: REVIEW THE SITUATION

List all the situations when your child typically uses their pacifier. Identifying these situations allows you to understand your child's underlying needs and can help you find alternatives. Make a table like the one below before beginning on your path to a pacifier-free life:

REASONS FOR PACIFIER	SUBSTITUTES
In the car	A bag of toys, a book, an audio story, a travel stuffed animal...
After an ouchie	A magic kiss, a special song...
When upset	Controlled breathing, coloring...

⭐ LISTEN AND DISCUSS

Don't try to hide your child's pacifier behind their back. This is a team effort, include them in the dialogue. Ask questions like "Why do you feel you need your pacifier?" and listen to their responses. Then, list advantages for getting rid of their pacifier (for their teeth, to be able to talk better, to feel more independent).

⭐ BE PATIENT

Living without a pacifier is a learning experience. Just like learning to walk or talk, it's progressive. There will be highs and lows...

⭐ TAKE BABY STEPS AND MAKE COMPROMISES

You don't have to ban binky all at once. Just be sure you're reducing overall usage and sticking to clearly defined rules. Start with small steps like "no more pacifier in the car, no more pacifier at nap time" until they're able to get rid of it completely!

⭐ BE POSITIVE

If your child can't let go of paci, don't force it. Failure is part of the journey. Focus on the progress: a couple minutes less each day is a success!

★ USE YOUR IMAGINATION

Pacita is a fairy-tale character and a useful tool to help support you and your child as you navigate this challenge. Use your imagination to bring the character lo life: decorate a magic "pacifier box" together or draw a picture of Pacita's great binky collection. Engaging your child in the process of separation makes it easier for everyone.

★ WRITE PACITA'S LETTERS

The letters from Pacita help you reinforce the separation process and give your child support at strategic milestones (when your child first gives up binky or after a couple tough days).
For greater impact, personalize your own letters.

Letter 1 Encouragement
● Objective: Emphasize the process.
● Tips: Highlight the skills required (patience, perseverance, courage, etc.) while adding words of comfort and solutions in case your child misses their pacifier. Sprinkle it with words that make them feel proud!

Letter 2 Compliment
● Objective: Emphasize the success.
● Tips: Write your congratulations and let your child know that they're growing up.

Download example letters at
**https://bigkidchronicles.com/
pacita-the-pacifier-fairy/**

★ BE FIRM

Parents are responsible for setting limits. Clear boundaries make a child feel secure. Once you've taken the pacifier, don't change your mind!

Be comforting but firm, that's the key!

AN EXPERT'S ADVICE

FROM AUDE MOUTON, FRENCH CLINICAL PSYCHOLOGIST

★ **What relationships does a child have with their pacifier?**

Above everything else, it's biological! Babies have a need to suck and a pacifier is a good substitute for mother's breast. Sucking encourages a release of hormones that lead to a feeling of well-being and pleasure. It's relaxing and soothing. It's therefore a response to a need for comfort.

★ **When does a pacifier become a problem?**

When it becomes the only response for dealing with emotions and frustration. For the child who needs a pacifier when they're tired, fearful, or sad; and for the parents who use it systematically to deal with tears, tantrums, or as a sleep aid.

★ **Is there a good time to stop using pacifiers?**

The right age is when the parent-child relationship is ready: when parents feel pacifier usage has become an interference, when they feel capable of handling the challenge, and when the child is able to respond positively to the change. If not, the change is unlikely to be adopted. It's important to take other developmental stages (like learning to walk, talk, or potty training) into account. You don't want to put too much pressure on the child all at once. Usually, a child should be perfectly capable of understanding and responding between 18 months and 2 years.

★ **Can we use presents as encouragement?**

With external rewards, the child is not able to think about the principles behind the behavior that we're asking them to change.

The neurological system of rewards brings a higher long term risk because as the child becomes an adolescent, they try to recreate this situation by seeking external validation from their peers. They absolutely need to understand the social necessity behind the new behavior and the internal rewards, which will help build a feeling of accomplishment (listening, affection, support, and congratulations).

One final tip: believe in your child!

★ Charlotte Attry (co-author)

A French author and journalist, Charlotte has been writing about psychological and social issues for twenty years. Charlotte holds a master's in literature from Paris La Sorbonne, a master's in Journalism, and a bachelor's in Psychology. She lives in California with her family.

★ Jeremie Febvre (co-author)

Developing original ideas, driving innovative projects, and fostering creativity have been the backbone of Jeremie's career over the past 20 years. The common thread that links his multiple ventures and collaborations is the neverending search for the right word. Jeremie is the proud father of Ava and Raphael, a hectic and joyful source of inspiration for the Big Kid Chronicles series.

★ Olivier Huette (illustrator)

"Drawing for children is like being five years old forever." For 15 years, Oliver has been bringing the wonderful worlds of children's books to life, with more than 30 books to his name. Despite his accomplishments, Olivier is still just as excited to take off on the next adventure: as a knight fighting dragons, a reckless pirate, or a sensitive little tiger!

★ Sophie Lawson (translator)

Sophie is passionate about the English language and loves everything from poetry to punctuation, which she studied at the University of California, Berkeley. Now a mother of two, Sophie is learning how to juggle her career and her family life. While she often finds herself swamped with work, she knows that it's never too late for a bedtime story!